NIGHT HAWKE

A SECOND GENERATION HAWKE FAMILY
PREQUEL

BILLIONAIRES OF NEW ORLEANS: THE HAWKE
FAMILY SECOND GENERATION

GWYN MCNAMEE

NIGHT HAWKE

© 2022 Gwyn McNamee

Cover Models: Andrew Biernat and Evan

Photographer: Wander Aguiar

Cover Design: Michelle Johnson at Bluesky Design

Editing: Stephie Walls at Wallflower Edits

1

ISAAC

There are few guarantees in life—death, taxes, and that the night is going to end with my dick buried inside that redhead across the bar.

God fucking willing...

She tosses back her head, laughing effortlessly at something her blond friend says, the sound light and airy. Sexy as fuck. It goes straight to my cock and makes it swell against my zipper.

What is a girl like that doing in a dive like this?

I shift on the stool, surreptitiously adjusting my semi, keeping my gaze locked on her. She casts a furtive glance at me out of the corner of her eye—at least the tenth time I've caught her doing so since Coen and I arrived almost an hour ago.

Her amber eyes meet mine for a split second, and the corner of her red lips twitches before she returns her focus to her friend at their small high-top near the pool table.

An energy radiates from her, a vibrancy and pull that makes me want to ditch Coen in favor of a much more interesting evening. After the last few months, nothing sounds better than celebrating my accomplishment with her under me, over me—however she wants it.

I raise my empty beer bottle to the bartender and incline my head, indicating I want another. He grabs one from the fridge and brings it over, sliding it across the marred wooden bar top to me.

"Thanks, man." I tilt it at him in recognition. "Hey"—I tip my head slightly toward the girl—"you know her?"

He follows my focus and shakes his head. "No. First time she's been in here. At least when I've been working. I would remember a girl like her."

No shit.

That isn't the type of girl you forget.

Her hair spills down past her exposed shoulders and over the cutout at the back of her skin-tight, short, black dress that shows off her curves and more of her flawless, alabaster skin.

She's the kind of woman who can burn you and you'd let her, just to be that close to the fire sparking in her eyes.

meantime..." I pull my keys from my pocket and hand them to him. "Head back to my place. I'm going to go talk to the redhead."

He smirks. "You're ditching me?"

"I'll be home in New Orleans permanently in two days. You're going to see plenty of me. So much that you'll probably get sick of me."

Coen examines the keys. "You're not going to try to bring the redhead back to your place tonight?"

I bark out a laugh and shake my head, tossing a couple twenties on the bar for our drinks. "No. Having your little brother hanging out at your condo kind of kills the mood."

"Gee, sorry I'm cock-blocking you."

I lean toward him and nudge his shoulder with mine. "You're not cock-blocking anything." I pull out my phone and swipe the screen. "I'm texting my friend, who is a concierge at the Palmer House. He'll have a room ready and waiting for me when I get her out of here."

"When?" Coen raises his brows. "Don't you mean *if*?"

I peek over my shoulder at her and meet her amber gaze again. "There is no *if*."

"Christ"—he releases a heavy laugh, pushing to his feet—"you're a dick."

Grinning at him, I waggle my eyebrows. "That may be, but I'm a dick who's going to spend some time with a beautiful woman tonight. Unlike you."

Coen shakes his head, smirking. "Asshole."

I push off from the bar, nudging the stool back, so I can slide out and move toward the redhead who now stands alone at the high-top, her back to me while she types on her phone. Her friend seems to have vanished while I was talking with Coen. I wave to Coen before he steps out the front door, and I approach the girl slowly so as not to startle her when she's so fully engrossed in whatever she's doing.

"Your friend abandoned you?"

She jerks slightly and turns to me as I move to the other side of the small, round table and set down my drink.

"Oh, no." A smile plays on her perfect lips, and she slips her phone into a small purse in front of her. "She had to take a phone call and wanted some privacy. She's just outside."

I *tsk* and shake my head, grinning at her. "Very dangerous of her to leave you like that. Haven't you seen the way the men in here look at you?"

She scans the almost empty bar now that Coen has slipped out. "I've seen the way *you* have been looking at me."

I take a sip of my beer, keeping my eyes on her. "How have I been looking at you?"

She leans her elbows on the table, flashing me her ample cleavage and twirling a strand of red hair around her finger. "The same way I've been looking at you."

Well, damn.

Direct. To the point. Not nervous or shy.

Never looked away from me for one second when she said it.

This is a woman who knows what she wants and takes it.

And fuck if that isn't the sexiest thing.

There's nothing hotter than a strong woman, and it's been far too long since I've met one. Though something tells me that no one I've *ever* met is anything like the one across the table from me. It's too bad I didn't meet her earlier, during my three years here in Chicago. She's different from the other girls I've spent my very little free time with. Stronger. More confident. Not looking to latch onto me for the wrong reasons.

This is pure animal attraction. What it's *supposed* to feel like. This is *wanting* something and being willing to bend over backward to get it. This woman is *special.*

She's a fantasy before me, a dream come to life.

Maybe the perfect woman.

And tonight, she's going to be mine.

————

JACK

THE MAN STANDING in front of me might just be the definition of walking sex. It oozes off him the same way the heavenly, masculine scent does, floating over the table to me, forcing me to inhale it with every breath. Crisp. Clean. It makes me want to bury my face in his shirt and never stop smelling it.

Something flutters deep inside me—a longing, a need I've never felt this strongly. It struck me the moment our eyes connected the first time and hasn't stopped during the hour Felicity and I have been here with him. And now that he's finally made his move, he's even more handsome up this close than he appeared sitting at the bar.

Striking Caribbean-blue eyes rake over me from under a mop of thick, dark, wavy hair. A playful smile tilts his lips, surrounded by rough stubble covering his powerful jaw.

He watches me with keen interest as I take a sip of my Jack and Coke to try to calm my racing heart while I think about what that would feel like between my thighs.

What the hell is wrong with me?

Flirting with a man has never unnerved me like this, but it may have something to do with the adrenaline coursing through my system from my "escape" today. I was already riding high and enjoying the freedom of my night away from everything before I ever stepped foot in this dive.

It just feels good to be out, to be normal, to be

sitting here, talking with a hot guy who seems as interested in me as I am in him, without knowing someone is watching me and reporting my every move to the people who can make my life a living hell and enjoy keeping me on a short leash.

The only person whose eyes I want on me now is across the table from me.

"You've been watching me. I've been watching you." He leans forward, resting his elbows on the table. "Seems we're on the same page. I just need to know what you'd like to do about it. Because I sure know what I'd like to do...and how."

His tongue darts out across his lips, his gaze darkening.

Sweet mother of God, that's hot.

I swallow through my suddenly dry throat and take another sip of my drink before I can speak again. "I have some ideas."

He chuckles. "I bet you do, sweetheart."

Sweetheart.

That should be insulting. It's condescending, misogynistic, and *should* make me want the punch him and tell him to go fuck himself. And I've certainly said and *done* worse to other men who have called me that...or worse. But instead, the little flutter in my chest at the pet name makes me lean in closer to him.

"*You* might be dangerous, though. A girl has to be careful."

He grins. "Oh, I'm definitely dangerous, and I

agree about being careful. I just graduated from law school, and I can tell you, there are definitely some unsavory and perverted men out there who do not have good intentions."

"Law school, huh?" My gaze dips to his lips, then back up. "That explains the silver tongue."

Something blazes across his eyes, a heat that roars through every cell of my body. "You have no idea what my tongue is capable of."

My entire body clenches, and I have to shift back slightly; otherwise, I'd be liable to throw myself across the tiny space separating us.

And that would be unwise.

I can't just rush out of here with a total stranger because I have a lady boner for him. The responsible and smart thing to do is at least assess him and the situation a little more. I motion over my shoulder. "How about we play a game of pool?"

He releases a deep laugh, the sound sexy and thick in a way that goes straight between my legs. Amusement flashes in his eyes. "Sure. You can break."

You can break.

The words seem to hold some sort of double meaning that keep his lips curled into a knowing smirk.

This man is most certainly *dangerous*; though, I don't think it has anything to do with the things girls are always warned about by their mothers. *This* man is dangerous in a way that will destroy your body and soul.

Standing, I take a sip of my drink, then grab a cue from the far wall while he wanders over from the high-top, watching my every move.

Examining the empty felt, I bite my bottom lip. "I forget how you start."

He fights a laugh and produces a triangle from somewhere under the table. "I'll rack them." He pulls out a ball and rolls it toward me. "You use the cue ball for breaking—the white one."

I lean forward to catch it, exposing my breasts to him slightly in the low *V* of my dress—a move he does not miss. His gaze dips with me, then he clears his throat, and I watch, mesmerized, as his strong hands place each ball meticulously.

Once satisfied, he pulls off the triangle and returns it to its original place. He motions toward the table and winks. "All yours, sweetheart. Do your worst."

It takes every ounce of willpower I have to hold back a smirk as I line up my shot, fumbling the cue slightly. I take a half-assed shot at the white ball, and it rolls lazily and barely bumps into the perfectly racked set-up.

He walks over to me and steps close, so close that the masculine scent completely dominates every breath I take. "Let's try that again." He grabs the cue ball and replaces it while I move back into position. "I'll help you this time."

I shift forward and line up my shot again, sticking my butt out behind me. He steps behind me, pressing his tall, hard, lean body against mine, his crotch pushed firmly to my ass. Leaning over me, his lips brush against my right ear, and he places his hands on top of mine on the cue, adjusting my grip.

"Now...slide it back gently and then forward with as much force as you can."

He drives his body into me as he says it, mimicking the motion, and I bite back a little groan at the magnificence of all that power. The men I've been with in the past have always held back, restrained themselves—either because they feared me or the repercussions of certain people discovering they were with me. But with him, I'm anonymous. Just a girl he met at a bar. Nothing is restricting him or me.

With his assistance, the cue ball launches forward and slams into the others, sending the four into the right corner pocket.

But he doesn't back away, just keeps his body molded to mine, his warm breath fluttering behind my ear. "That was much better."

"Thank you."

He trails a hand along my bare arm, sending goosebumps skittering over my skin. "So, are you going to tell me your name?"

I turn my head toward his until our lips are a mere

hairsbreadth apart. "I'll tell you my name if you can beat me at pool."

Taking a half-step back, he barks out a laugh and nods. "It's a deal." He motions toward the table. "You think you can handle your next shot by yourself?"

Again, I fight the smile that so desperately wants to spread across my lips. "I think I can handle it."

He retreats a step and sweeps out his arm for me to move in front of him and make my way around the table. I examine the options on the felt, then send the two easily into the far-left corner pocket. Shifting to my left to where the cue ball rolled, I quickly do the same to the five and seven into the right and side pockets. I knock down the three and six next, then aim for the one, my last remaining solid, but it ricochets just to the right of the pocket, breaking my run.

With an annoyed huff, I rise from my slumped position on the table to find him staring at me, his eyes hooded and dark with something I can't quite figure out.

Definitely not anger.

It almost looks like he's impressed.

He inclines his head toward the table. "You're a shark."

I lean against the cue, feigning innocence. "Excuse me?"

He grins and approaches slowly, like a panther stalking its helpless prey, waiting to pounce, and stops in front of me. With our gazes locked, he wraps his hand around mine on the cue, the contact sending a sizzle of heat through my arm and between my legs.

"I said"—he leans closer—"you're a shark. You played me."

This time, I don't fight the satisfied smirk. "Maybe."

"Who taught you how to play like that?"

"My dad."

He nods slowly. "So, you have no intention of giving me your name, then?"

I chuckle and shake my head. "It's probably better that we don't do that whole thing, right?"

If I told him, it would change everything, and this flirtatious banter is working up to something that will be combustible. I don't want anything to interfere with that. Finding out who I am would be like throwing a bucket of ice water on this smolder, and that's the last thing I want.

A good *explosive* release would do us both some good, I think.

Those blue eyes watch me for a second, trying to process my words. "Yeah, you're right."

"But you can call me Jack."

One of his dark brows rises. "Jack, hmm?" His gaze darts over to the Jack and Coke on the table. "Creative."

He's quiet for a moment, likely trying to come up with something as "clever" as the name I just gave him. "You can call me Nolan."

"Nolan, huh?"

"Uh-huh."

It isn't his real name, and I don't want it, anyway. This can never be anything more than one night, so there isn't any use in getting to know each other like that. Anonymity is the only thing keeping me from being dragged back to the last place I want to be right now. There's a reason we chose this bar tonight—because it's the last place *they'd* ever look for me.

Tonight, I can just be Jack.

"So, Jack"—he steps into me until our chests brush against each other, tightening his hand on mine around the smooth wood. "Now that you've handed my ass to me, I don't think we need to finish the game, do you? It's time we get out of here."

"Oh, you think so?"

"I do." He nods toward the door of the bar. "You notice your friend hasn't even come back for you?"

What?

It takes a second for me to process what he just said.

Where the hell is Felicity?

I rush back to the table and pull out the burner phone I've been using today to find a text from her.

FELICITY

> BOBBY JUST CAME AND PICKED
> ME UP. I STUCK MY HEAD IN AND
> SAW YOU WITH THAT GUY WE
> WERE TALKING ABOUT, SO I
> FIGURED YOU'RE OKAY. LET ME
> KNOW IF YOU WANT ME TO COME
> BACK AND PICK YOU UP. WE CAN
> BE THERE IN FIVE MINUTES.

Am I okay?

Going home with a total stranger is about as irresponsible an idea as I've ever had—one Mom and Dad would certainly completely lose their shit over—but there's something about him, something I can't ignore.

This might be my one night of freedom. I can't let this opportunity go. Not when they'll never let this happen again.

I text her back.

JACK

> I'm okay. I'll let you know where I am
> and send you proof of life in the
> morning.

She replies almost instantly.

FELICITY

> GO GET SOME BEFORE YOUR
> PARENTS LOCK YOU BACK UP
> AGAIN!

I let out a laugh at her words of encouragement and turn back to face Nolan. He leans against the pool table, observing everything but giving me space.

His brow furrows with concern. "She good?"

Nodding, I push the phone back into my purse. "She's with her boyfriend. He only lives a few blocks from here. He was going to meet us, but he just picked her up instead."

"What about you? Are you good?"

Such a loaded question.

Things haven't felt "good" in such a long time, but tonight, the brief time I've spent with him has given me a sense of freedom and *rightness* I can't remember ever experiencing.

I smile at him and grab my purse. "I will be when we get out of here."

A grin spreads across his lips, and he steps forward and holds out his hand. I slip mine into it, and the heat from his firm grip warms me from the inside out. Despite that, a shiver rolls through me. Anticipation of knowing what's coming and how good it's going to be.

If it is only for one night, I'm going to enjoy the hell out of it.

2

JACK

We step out of the bar onto the street, and the cool, early spring wind whips off Lake Michigan and down around us, sending a chill through me. I shiver slightly, the open-backed, short dress not giving me much protection from the feature that gave this city its nickname.

Nolan wraps a muscular arm around me and pulls me to his side, glancing at his phone. "Our ride will be here in one minute."

The heat of his hard body pressed against mine relieves some of the chill—so does knowing what will happen as soon as we get into that car. This sizzling charge between us sparks like fireworks in the night as I gaze up at him, again imagining how that strong jaw covered in a well-groomed beard would abrade my thighs.

My fingers itch to run through the dark, unruly hair blowing in the breeze, but before I can reach up to grab it, a black Town Car pulls up at the curb.

Nolan ushers me toward it with a gentle hand on my back.

I raise an eyebrow. "Wow. Fancy."

He chuckles. "I thought I'd spring for the upgrade tonight."

"Trying to impress me?"

A slow smile spreads across his lips as he opens the door for me. "Do I need to?"

Instead of answering him, I just give a sly smile and climb inside, sliding across the plush leather seat. Nolan follows, closing the door behind him, and the driver glances over his shoulder at us through an open privacy window.

"Palmer House?"

Nolan nods. "Yes, thank you."

He reaches forward, slides the window closed, then draws me next to him, his body pushed against mine. We pull away from the curb and head toward the loop, and he stares out the window with an almost forlorn look in his eyes, so different from the playful and flirty attitude he's had so far this evening.

"It really is a beautiful city."

His words hold a melancholy that makes an ache form in my chest. I look out the window, too, trying to see what he does, instead of the place I feel trapped in.

"It can be. It can also be dirty, violent, and harsh."

He offers a sad smile. "That's all true, too, even so, I'm going to miss it."

Miss it?

"You're leaving?"

It shouldn't matter. After tomorrow morning, I won't ever see him again, regardless of whether he's in Chicago or not. Still, the words make me shift restlessly on the seat.

"Yeah." He brushes his fingers across my exposed arm slowly. "I leave Sunday. Now that I'm done with law school, it's time to return home."

I don't ask him where home is, even though the question sits on the tip of my tongue. "Wow. Not hanging around too long. Huh?"

Nolan shakes his head. "We have a family business. Well, a lot of them, actually. And my father is the attorney for all of it. Dealing with the family shit is *more* than a full-time job. He really needs me there." His hand stills against my skin, and he gets a faraway look for a moment, like he's seeing his future. "I'll take the bar in July and will start appearing in court as soon as I'm sworn in, but there's enough for me to do in the meantime that doesn't require me to have my license yet. Dad needs my help."

It sounds like it's all laid out nicely for him—so different from where I find myself, constantly wondering what my life can be when it feels like a noose keeps tightening around my neck.

"Shouldn't you be packing instead of hanging out with me tonight?"

He lowers his head to mine, grazing his lips against my ear. "There's no place else I'd rather be." Pulling his head back, he grins. "Besides, I already have my place packed up and the movers scheduled to come Monday. My landlord will let them in and get them sent on their way."

"Wow. Anxious to get home, then?"

Something flashes across his eyes—a look of longing mixed with trepidation, and he offers me a tight smile. "Sort of. My family can be...demanding."

I chuckle and shake my head, pushing my hair back behind my ear. "I feel you on that. I've lived here my whole life under the very watchful eye of my parents, who treat me like a child no matter how old I get."

He raises his eyebrows. "You don't seem like the type to let anyone keep you on a leash."

I interlock my fingers with his, where they rest against my exposed thigh. "I appreciate you saying that, but really, it's a constant battle. More often than not, I lose."

"I'm surprised you lose at anything after the way you just ran that table."

That draws a laugh from my throat, and I shrug. "To be honest, some of my parents' concerns are warranted, so it's hard to fight them on certain things."

He nods, but no one will ever be able to understand it unless they live it. And no one lives the way I do. No one should *have* to. I won't waste my breath, trying to explain it to Nolan, though. It would give away too much, and tonight isn't about any of that.

We stop at a red light on the corner near the Chicago Cultural Center, and he leans forward slightly, staring up at it.

"Do you know the history of the Cultural Center building?"

I glance at it as we pass. "Yeah. Fascinating, isn't it?"

"The history and architecture here are two of the reasons I chose Chicago to come to law school when I had plenty of other options. There's just something about these old buildings that draws me to them."

Another question sits on the tip of my tongue, but I swallow it back.

Don't delve too deep.

Getting too interested in the man I'm walking away from in a few hours isn't a good idea. I curl my fingers into my hand to stop myself from asking and instead focus on the other major draw to this city. "Do you ever spend any time down by the lake?"

He chuckles and shakes his head. "Not much— other than the occasional run along the shoreline.

While Lake Michigan is beautiful, it doesn't hold a candle to what I'm used to."

"You're a water guy?"

"My father and uncles own a boat. It's big enough to take extended trips out to open water to do some fishing."

"How big is it?"

His gaze heats, and he waggles his eyebrows. "Wouldn't you like to know..."

I playfully swat at his arm. "Knock it off. I meant the *boat.*"

"About seventy feet."

"That's more like a yacht."

"I guess." He shifts, seemingly uncomfortable with the topic of conversation, almost like he doesn't want me to know the kind of money his family has. Like it would somehow change things. He's hiding behind the name Nolan the same way I am with Jack.

Still, he's opened the door to the obvious question. "So, you're rich?"

He barks out a laugh that's a little too loud for the car. "*I'm* not rich. My *family* is. I never really considered it my money. They all worked very hard for what they have, and I'm going to have to do the same now that I'm stepping into my role."

I appreciate his answer more than I would like to admit. He's a hard worker and wants to earn what he gets in life. That's admirable. Yet, the way he says "stepping into my role" sounds more like he's being forced into it.

"You don't seem too happy about that, to be stepping into that role."

He shakes his head. "No. It's not that. It's just...I've been working toward this for so long that it's hard to wrap my head around the fact that it's finally here." He stares out the window again. "What about you? Are you going into the family business?"

I shake my head, clenching my jaw against the desire to rant about the family obligations and expectations that made me flee them and brought me to him tonight. "I'm not allowed to."

His head whips toward mine, blue eyes wide. "*Allowed* to?"

"I told you it's complicated."

He takes my hand in his and pulls it to his lips. "We're going to uncomplicate things, at least for a while." He presses light kisses across the back of my smooth skin, sending butterflies flying in my stomach, then leans in and brushes his lips against my ear again. "Let's forget all this bullshit tonight."

I turn my head toward his slightly, our lips only a millimeter away from each other. "That sounds good to me."

More than good.

Fucking fantastic.

I wait for him to press his lips to mine, for what I've been longing for him to do, what I know we both have craved the entire time we were inside that bar. But he doesn't give me what I want. He retreats with a knowing smirk and settles back in his seat as we finally pull up outside the Palmer House.

Nolan slips from the car and waits to help me do the same. I place my palm in his extended hand, and he squeezes with a firm grip, pulling me up and into his arms.

The warm strength surrounding me makes me sag against him, and he grins at me.

"You ready, Jack?"

"More than ready..."

ISAAC

THE WIND WHIPS off Lake Michigan, funneling down Monroe Street, swirling Jack's vibrant red hair around her face like a blazing halo.

Only she's no angel.

Far from it.

More like walking sin designed to test my restraint and push me to the limits of my control.

The moment I slid into that Town Car and closed the door behind me, sealing me in with her, all I wanted to do was pin her to the expensive leather and drive into her until we both forgot who we were and only *felt.*

Keeping my hands and mouth to myself was nearly impossible, but now that we're so close to the ultimate payoff, I pull her close to me and tuck her hair behind her ear, staring down into the vibrant amber eyes that hold the same desire roaring through me right now.

Lowering my head, I press my lips to her cheek. "Let's get you inside and warmed up."

Her hands tighten around me, and I encircle her with my arm to guide her toward the front doors of the Palmer House and a night I'm sure to remember for the rest of my life. She's not the type of girl you can forget, regardless of how hard you try. Even if she had rejected me and I had left the bar alone, the image of her examining me from across the room would have stuck with me.

Once I get my hands on her, I won't forget how she feels or the sounds she makes as I plunge into her. It will be one hell of a way to remember my last weekend in Chicago.

We step through the innocuous exterior entry and face the *true* doors the Palmer House is famous for. Ornate, ten-foot bronze peacocks designed by Tiffany and Co. welcome us, supposedly worth over a million dollars, only a brief glimpse of the grandeur to come when we climb the stairs to the main lobby.

Having a woman this beautiful on my arm in a place this incredible almost seems like a dream.

One I'm not sure I ever want to wake up from.

To already have that thought when I've barely touched her makes my chest tighten, but I push away that apprehension in favor of leading her up the steps to the lobby. At the top, she pauses and sucks in a tiny breath, her wide eyes scanning the vast, austere room.

I wrap my arm around her waist from behind and tug her back against me, nuzzling her neck. "We can go sit at the bar and have a few more drinks, pretend to talk when we both really just want to get into the elevator and head up to the room..."

She turns her head toward me, her lips grazing my cheek, and rests her hands on top of mine, her small purse dangling from one. "Let's get a drink."

The sly tilt of her lips as she pulls out of my hold makes my cock twitch. Here I thought I was toying with her in the car, keeping her waiting for what she wants, but she's been playing me since the moment we met—first running the pool table and now leaving me hanging the same way I did her.

That's fine, though. I love to play games, especially with an opponent like Jack and when I know what I'll win in the end. Finally driving my cock into her slick heat will be worth the pursuit.

I grin at her and incline my head toward the bar. Jack moves ahead of me, intentionally swaying her shapely hips in the little black dress, her heels clicking on the marble. She glances over her shoulder to ensure I'm following and watching, mischief sparking in her eyes.

This woman is trouble. No doubt about it. But it's exactly the kind of trouble I need tonight.

Jack reaches the main lobby bar and slides onto a stool. Rather than taking a seat beside her, I lean against the bar and nod to the bartender.

He approaches with a friendly smile, tossing a towel over his shoulder. "What can I get for you?"

The feisty redhead who has my entire body coiled and ready to blow leans across the bar toward him slightly, flashing a sweet smile. "I'll have a Jack and Coke."

I chuckle again at her choice of fake name. "Give me a Blanton's neat."

Our bartender hurries off to make our order, and Jack spins on the stool toward me, uncrossing and recrossing her legs—the smooth expanse of exposed skin making my fingers itch to touch her.

She scans the lobby and focuses on the Louis Pierre Rigal mural on the ceiling. "This really is incredible."

I step forward between her legs, sliding my hands across her thighs to widen them, and her warm body practically hums against mine. "I'm surprised you've never been here before since you've always lived in the city."

A mirthless laugh falls from her lips as she stares up. "It isn't really my family's vibe."

Her mysterious comments about her family shouldn't bother me so much. We made a deal to leave the outside world there tonight and not to worry about it. But Jack is so opinionated, so direct that I have a hard time wrapping my head around her easily complying with parents who try to control her life. "You're what...twenty-two? Why not just leave if you don't want to be here, if you don't want to deal with the way your parents treat you?"

She returns her focus to me, lips pressed into a tight line. "Like I said, it's complicated." Her hands shift up my body, pressing against my abs and up to my chest as she tightens her legs around me. "But tonight doesn't have to be."

No. It doesn't.

It seems both of us need the same thing—an escape. And we can find it in each other for a brief moment in time before I face my future in NOLA and she returns to whatever complications weigh on her with her family here.

I nod. "Then, we're in agreement."

The bartender reappears and slides our drinks across to us.

Jack takes hers in hand and points toward the sign showing the way to the registration desk. "Don't you have to go check in?"

I shake my head, picking up my drink. "No. Digital check-in on my phone. As soon as we're finished with these drinks, we can go right up."

She fights a smile and takes a dainty little sip from her glass.

More games. More drawing out the tension and torture.

I lean in until my lips almost meet hers. "If you drink like that, we're never going to make it to the good part."

She turns her head and flutters her lips against my ear, and I trail my fingers lightly down her arm. All the brief touches. The near kisses. The heated looks. All of it is building to something sure to be extraordinary.

Her legs spread wider, allowing me to press my already growing cock between them, exactly where we both want it. I bite back a groan at the contact and take a sip of my bourbon, letting the sweet liquid glide down my throat and warm my gut.

Intense eyes watch me, focusing on my lips and dropping down my neck as I swallow. A flush spreads across her cheeks, and she brings her tumbler up but pauses coyly before she does anything with it.

Are we going to keep toying with each other, or is Jack finally ready to unleash what's bottled up inside us both?

She puts her glass to her lips, tilts her head back, and downs the entire thing in two quick gulps. "We better hurry, then."

Fuck yes.

I down the rest of my drink, set the empty crystal tumbler on the bar, and toss a hundred-dollar bill next to it for the bartender. It's far more than our bill could be, but I refuse to wait another minute to get my hands on Jack.

He just got a hefty tip for very little work, but I'm the one winning tonight. I take Jack's hand and tug her off the stool to stand in front of me. Her hips brush against my growing cock, and I bury my hand in her hair and tug her head back slightly to look up at me.

Her lust-soaked gaze tells me everything I need to know.

3
_____

JACK

As soon as the elevator doors slide open, Nolan ushers me in with a hand at my lower back, just above my ass—low enough to be sexual but not obscene. It's yet another delicate touch intended to build the tension between us and drive me absolutely mad.

The entire cab ride over here...

His knee brushing mine...

His fingers trailing along my bare thigh and arm...

But nothing more.

Not even a feather of a kiss.

And it's intentional. Some sort of game to him. A way to make me desperate and needy before we ever reached the hotel room. And it's fucking working. Far better than I want to admit.

It's outright torture.

Just the way he held my hand walking to the lobby was enough to make me clench my thighs.

So dominant.

Protective.

Possessive.

No man has ever done this to me before, has ever elicited this rush. This thrill. This desperation. And I wanted him to feel it, too. But all my little game at the bar did was make me need him more. He's so passionate, so intense, and I want all that passion and intensity focused on me.

And now, we're finally alone in this tight, enclosed space.

Nothing but the air and sexual tension filling it.

He cages me against the wall of the pristine, elegant elevator, then reaches over and presses the button for the twentieth floor. Only he doesn't stop there, just slowly trails his fingers down to light up every single floor between the lobby and where our room waits for us.

"What are you doing?"

A slow, devious grin spreads across the lips I've been fantasizing about having on me since the moment I saw him at the bar. It spells nothing but danger. "I want more time with you in here."

Oh, sweet mother of God. I'm in trouble.

He brushes his lips lightly over mine. Barely a whisper. Barely a touch. Barely even there. But it lights a fire in my core that has me gripping the lapels of his suit coat to keep my knees from buckling.

I suck in a shaky breath. "We could have gotten to the room faster if you hadn't done that."

He chuckles against my lips. "What fun would that be?"

His right hand slips between my thighs and up under my dress.

I tighten my grip on him. "Nolan"—I glance up at the camera in the elevator's corner—"someone will see us."

The doors slide closed, and the car begins to move up, his hand mimicking the motion.

"That's the entire point, Jack."

His lips crash to mine, robbing me of my ability to respond with anything coherent. He devours me with a feral hunger that matches my own, the sweet taste of the bourbon he was drinking hitting my tongue.

Strong, determined fingers find the thin strip of material covering my pussy, and he groans into my mouth. "Christ, Jack, you're already soaking wet."

I pant against his lips, tugging on his jacket. "What did you expect? After that little performance in the car back there and then at the bar."

The elevator jerks to a stop, and the doors open. I nervously turn my head to check the hallway outside on the second floor, but thankfully, no one's waiting.

Gripping my chin with his free hand, Nolan turns my face back to him and kisses me deeply again, probing his tongue along mine, his fingers slipping aside my thong and plunging into me.

"You liked that, though, didn't you?" The doors to the elevator close. "Just like you like this." He probes deeper inside me, and the car moves up again. "The fact that someone's watching us."

I don't want to admit he's right, but my body clenches around his fingers in response. His chest rumbles in satisfaction as he pumps inside me, his thumb finally finding my throbbing clit.

The elevator stops again, the doors opening ominously. If we get caught, we'll get kicked out before we ever get to the room.

And that would be a real fucking tragedy.

Our exposure doesn't stop Nolan, though; he continues kissing me while languidly stroking my pussy.

This isn't a race.

Long, drawn-out strokes inside me.

Slow, deliberately gentle, almost glancing swipes over my clit.

As floor after floor passes, the doors opening and closing again, he only winds me up tighter. My arousal coats the inside of my thighs, slick against his hand.

If this is what he can do with *that*, I can't even *imagine* what he can do with his mouth and other assets. That silver tongue coils and strokes mine the higher we climb, mimicking what his expert fingers are doing.

But every time I start to get that little buzz coursing through my veins, that heat spreading across my skin, every time I get even remotely close to coming, he pulls me back again, dangling my orgasm just out of reach, relentless in both his drive and his restraint.

The elevator halts at the next floor—at this point, I've completely lost track of where we are—and the doors open, but neither of us has bothered to check for anyone the last few times.

"Oh, *whoops...*"

The startled voice from the hallway just outside the open doors makes me jerk my head away from Nolan's in time to see a white-haired woman back away, but Nolan doesn't even acknowledge the interruption. He just moves his kisses to my neck and keeps working me over with his dexterous digits.

"Ma'am, I'm sorry. I—"

Nolan silences me with his lips, drawing out a groan from deep in my chest. "Let her watch..."

Oh, hell.

My pussy clamps down on his fingers, and he keeps going as the doors shut. I peek at the floor indicator panel.

Thank God.

One more floor.

I can't take much more of this. If we had to keep moving up at such an agonizingly slow rate, I might end up fucking him right here in the elevator. And while the thought that security is likely watching us is somehow making my pussy drip like a faucet, that doesn't necessarily mean I want to ride Nolan in the elevator of one of the swankiest hotels in Chicago for everyone to see.

Okay, that's a lie. I do...

I so, so do.

The final ding and opening of the doors send a relieved breath whooshing from my lungs.

This torture is finally over.

Only instead of pulling his hand from between my thighs, he wraps his other arm around my waist and drags me against him. His stiff cock presses against my leg. He turns me and walks me backward out of the elevator and into the hall—fingers still buried inside me, thumb still moving slowly across my clit in a way he has to know is killing me.

My back hits something hard, and I pull away from his kiss to glance behind me at the door. "Our room?"

He inclines his head, while still stroking me, unrelenting. "The King Suite."

"Ar-aren't you going to open the door?"

A lecherous grin curls his lips. "I have something else in mind, sweetheart."

"What?" The single word comes out so breathy, it's

barely audible. If he weren't literally on top of me, there's no way he would have heard it.

"You're so fucking wet, drenching my hand at the thought of all those people watching us on the cameras in the elevator." He softly kisses the corner of my lips. "You should have felt the way your body reacted when that woman tried to come in." He shakes his head with a soft chuckle. "You fucking gushed. Nothing fucking sexier." He pulls his fingers out of me and holds them up, glistening in the hallway's light. "And now, I can't wait to taste you."

I stand against the door, panting, my body quivering, and Nolan slips his wet digits into his mouth, licking and sucking off all the evidence of how fucking turned on I really was—*am*—by what just happened.

God, that's hot.

His tongue darts out across his wet lips then he leans forward and kisses me deeply, the flavor of my own arousal filling my mouth. I cling to him, my body throbbing and grasping for something he isn't giving me.

He pulls back and lowers himself to his knees, leaving my hands on his shoulders.

"What the hell are you doing?" I glance up and down the empty hallway as he kisses my belly and makes his way lower, his hands tugging up the hem of my dress.

"I'm going to eat you until you come down my

throat and I'm drowning in it. And then, I'll take you inside that room and fuck you so hard on every surface that you won't be able to move tomorrow."

Holy fucking hell.

Nolan looks up at me as he rips my lace thong completely apart, fully exposing me to him in the hallway.

I raise my brows at him. "*Here?*"

"Right fucking here, Jack."

ISAAC

THE SCENT of her cunt so fucking close to my face, combined with the small taste of her I got from my fingers, makes my mouth water and my cock twitch in the confines of my pants. If they weren't made of such expensive material, it might bust straight through it, demanding I give it what it wants.

And it wants *her*.

Fucking bad.

All of me does.

This woman has to be the sexiest fucking thing I've ever seen in my life.

Stunningly beautiful. Adventurous. Responsive. So willing to do whatever just feels good. Like this. And that's what tonight is all about—feeling good.

Enjoying what little time we have together before we go our separate ways.

With her standing in front of me, legs spread, bare, shaved pussy only centimeters from my face, there's no doubt I'll be able to completely lose myself in her tonight.

Starting now. I can't wait any longer, not when my cock throbs to be buried in her wet heat. I lower my head and glide my tongue through her wet lips.

"Oh, fuck!" Her hands delve into my hair, tightening and tugging on the strands. "Please, Nolan..."

I've barely touched her, only given her one swipe of my tongue, and she's already coiled and begging. We've been dancing around this, building up to it all night, and both of us are primed.

I pause and look up at her, her hooded eyes glowing with need. "Please, what? Please make me come, or please stop?"

It's not that I don't know the answer to that question, but I want to hear her say it. I *need* to hear her say it. The confirmation that she's one hundred percent on board with this even though her body is saying it.

She drops her head back against the door and squeezes her eyes closed, panting. "Fuck...make me come...make me come..."

Her words are so needy and desperate, matching the feeling gripping my body. Only my extremely well-practiced restraint used in the courtroom keeps me from whipping out my cock and fucking her right here, right now. That, and how fucking good she tastes.

So fucking good...

I can't stop, no matter how badly I may want to do countless other depraved things with her. Not when doing this out here, exposed to anyone who might walk down the hallway or be watching on the surveillance cameras is driving her absolutely mad.

Fingers twist in my hair.

Legs shake.

Hips thrust toward me, seeking.

I probe my tongue into her again, licking and sucking at the moisture already pooled there from what I did to her in the elevator. She's close. Damn close. I slip my fingers back inside to pump into her, steadier and faster than before.

And as much fun as our games have been, I don't want to toy with her anymore. Now I want—*no, need*—to make her come, to experience the rush of her release against my lips and in my mouth, swallowing it down, taking it all.

I haven't even been inside her yet, and already, it's like an addiction—an obsession to drink her in any way I can while I still have her here. Because something tells me she'll bolt as soon as we're through. Neither of us wants to do the awkward morning-after thing, but I suspect one night with her won't be enough. I'll want one more.

She squeezes around my fingers, gasping and banging her head back against the door, exposing her long, elegant neck. Her hands tighten on my hair almost painfully, and I suck her clit between my lips and pulse gently. Hips fly forward and slam against my face, her beautiful, lush thighs practically suffocating me with a violent squeeze—but I would die a happy man buried between her legs. I might have more than a few things to atone for with my maker, but it would all be worth it. Every last fucking second of it.

The harder I stroke at that perfect spot deep inside her, the louder she moans and the tighter her grip on my hair becomes. Her legs shake violently—so hard that only my shoulders pinning her to the door keep her upright. She's right there, right at the edge, and I'm close to blowing my fucking load in my pants.

I roll my tongue around her clit and bite down sharply.

She parts her beautiful lips on a gasp. "Oh, fuck!"

Her cunt clasps my fingers, and she explodes, her release rushing out of her and down my throat in a wave of liquid. I swallow all of it—every last fucking drop as she shakes and spasms. Missing any of it would be a sin, and I've already committed so many of those.

Christ. Jack squirting is the hottest thing I've ever seen in my fucking life.

She gasps again, her body twisting and contorting with the force of her orgasm, until she finally sags back against the door, panting. I languidly glide my tongue up each of her wet thighs and across her engorged clit. She jerks back from the sensation, and I pull away from her heated flesh and look up at her.

With her gorgeous, plump bottom lip pulled between her teeth, she peeks down at me with hooded eyes that hold concern and embarrassment instead of the typical relief they should. "I'm so sorry. I don't know what the hell that was…"

I push to my feet and capture her mouth with mine, silencing her distress the best way I can. Her hands find my jacket lapels, and she clings to me, letting me explore her mouth again the way I just did her pussy.

My cock twitches hard against my zipper, begging for release, but there's something I have to take care of first.

No fucking way I'll allow Jack to be embarrassed by what just happened.

She likely didn't know her body could do that, that a man could do that to *her*, so she doesn't understand what a big fucking turn-on it is for me to know I'm the one who worked her over and made her come harder than she ever has in her entire life.

It's a heady knowledge, and pride swells in my chest.

I was her first…

If for no other reason, she'll always remember what I did to her in this hallway, how I made her feel, and it's *nothing* she should ever have negative feelings about. Far from it.

I drag my head back from hers and glide my still-wet fingers across her lips slowly. "That's all you, sweetheart. And it's hot as hell. Don't ever be embarrassed about coming like that."

Her gaze softens, her cheeks reddening even more before her tongue darts out and slides along my fingers. A little groan comes up my throat imagining her mouth on my cock, and I press my body against hers as I fumble for my phone to scan the digital key card and get us into the room.

"Now, get ready, Jack, because that was only the beginning."

I have plans for this woman tonight, ones that will cement this rendezvous in both our minds for eternity.

4

ISAAC

I manage to get the door open, my lips still on hers, one hand clutching her hip, and walk her backward into the suite. The door slams closed behind us. She jerks away from my kiss and slips from my arms, scanning the room, her eyes a little unfocused.

"Wow. This is huge."

Smirking, I motion to the left. "Down there is a conference room, and that way"—I point to the right —"there is another seating area with a bar, and"—I point to another hallway—"over there is the south wing with the bedroom."

Her dark brows rise. "It has wings?"

I nod, chuckling. "It sure does...and so many

surfaces I can do so many nasty things to you on all night."

Her already-pink cheeks flame even more, and she offers a light, soft laugh. "I'm not sure I can handle much more."

I approach her slowly and grab her hips, dragging her back against me. "Oh, I *know* you can."

"You have so much faith in me."

The words seem to hold something heavy in them, something completely unrelated to what's happening between us. A reference to something she's trying to escape from tonight with me. And I'm more than willing to let her find whatever she needs in any way she wants.

I cup her cheek, tilting her face up to mine. "I may not know your real name, but given the way you smoked me at pool and how you responded in the elevator and hallway, I already know you're strong and don't back down from a challenge." I ghost my lips across hers. "I have unlimited faith in you, and I guarantee you're going to enjoy what I have in mind."

Jack wraps her hands around my neck, twisting the hair at my nape in her fingers, a smile playing on her lips. "And I have a feeling you're the kind of man who does everything well or dies trying. So...do your worst..."

"Oh, sweetheart, you have no idea what you're asking for."

After the couple of weeks I've had—exams,

packing up the condo to move back home, and dealing with the impending massive shift in my life—the pent-up tension has me ready to snap. And this woman is the perfect outlet for all of it.

Willing. Wanting. Beautiful.

Exactly what I needed tonight.

I easily lift her, and she wraps her legs around my waist, pressing herself against my rock-hard cock. Her heat sears me even through the fabric, and that contact alone is enough for me to grit my teeth to stop myself from coming in my pants. I walk us toward the chaise along the room's eastern wall under the window that would have given us a magnificent view of Lake Michigan back when this hotel was originally built.

But the only view I'm interested in now is of the woman in my arms. She stares at me with a passion burning in her eyes—the amber sparking with gold and red.

I slowly lower her to the soft fabric and lean down, grinding my erection against the apex of her thighs. She moans and tightens her grip on my neck, rolling her hips against me.

We kiss like it's our oxygen, like it's our life force, like there's no tomorrow, because, for us, there won't be. There's only tonight. There's only *now* and this feeling consuming us.

My entire body vibrates with barely restrained need. Every little noise of pleasure and frustration she makes only drives me to push her harder, to demand more from her. Because she *can* take it. What happened in the hallway surprised her, and there's more where that came from. She really doesn't understand what she asked for or what she's about to receive.

I drag my head back from hers and tug at the hem of her dress, pulling the black fabric up over her exposed core, her taut stomach, and finally exposing her pert breasts.

Fuck.

No bra.

This woman is trying to destroy me.

Tugging her dress over her head with one hand, I drop down to suck one hard, stiff, pink peak into my mouth. She arches up, rubbing against me with a little mewl, hands clinging to the back of my neck. Her skin burns against mine, searing it with the heat of her desire for this. For me. For the very thing I want so badly and have since the moment I saw her.

I release her nipple with a soft pop and kiss my way across her chest to give the other one the same treatment. Her warm skin pressed against my lips makes my cock ache, and the wetness between her thighs soaks the front of my pants. If I'm not careful, I'll only add to that mess in a second.

Things have been so hectic, so chaotic that my body is wound up tight and ready to blow at any moment.

Keep it together, Isaac.

Nothing could be more embarrassing than coming like a teenager with a woman like this. I need to make this last, but with her spread out under me, her pert nipple in my mouth, luscious body pressed to me, that's going to be impossible.

Reluctantly, I climb to my feet. She watches me from under long, dark lashes, her chest rising and falling rapidly, her pussy glistening in the moonlight streaming in from the windows. I reach for my belt buckle, and she slowly slips her right hand across her stomach and between her legs.

Fucking Christ...

And here I thought this woman couldn't get any hotter.

Jack drags her finger through her slit and up around her clit, biting her bottom lip on a moan. I quickly shove off my jacket, then unbutton my shirt and toss it to the floor. Gritting my teeth to keep from blowing my load, I manage to kick off my pants and boxers to take my hard, aching cock in my hand.

Thank fuck.

I stroke it a few times, my eyes darting between her heated gaze and what she's doing between her legs. "You're fucking stunning, Jack."

She releases her lip from between her teeth and assesses me with an approving gaze, her focus slowly drifting over my chest and stomach, then dropping to where my hand is wrapped around my dick. "So are you."

The appreciation in her assessment only makes me want to ravage her more. Her tongue darts across her lips as she locks her gaze on my cock. I grab a condom from my wallet and tear it open with my teeth while she continues to play with herself unabashedly. Coming the way she did in the hallway may have embarrassed her, but this is something she's done before. Something she's comfortable with. She isn't afraid to give herself pleasure or to take what she needs from me.

I can't get my dick wrapped up fast enough, then I climb over her and settle between her legs. She pulls away her hand, and I brush the head of my cock across her clit. Her body jerks at the contact, and she kicks off her heels, wraps her legs around me, and urges me forward with pressure on my lower back. I drag my cock across her most sensitive spot again, pressing down to provide friction that makes goose-bumps pebble across her sweat-dampened skin.

Her nails dig into my shoulders, and she shifts her hips, gliding my length between her legs, coating it in her wetness.

Fuck.

I grasp my cock tightly and align it with her slick opening, but even as wet as she is, it's going to stretch her open, take a little work for her to accept my size. She sucks in a shaky breath, meets my gaze, and I ease inside her slowly, spreading her pussy wide as it struggles to accept me.

She throws her head back, arching into me. "Oh, *Gooooodddddd.*"

I'd much rather she were saying my name—my real one—but she was right that it would have only complicated things. Our anonymity makes it so much easier to just let go, to let things happen and just *feel.*

And there's nothing I'd rather feel than her hot cunt gripping my cock.

I drive my hips forward, fully impaling her on me, clenching my jaw against the almost instant desire to come.

She gasps, clawing the back of my neck. "Oh, God."

Before I really get going, I need to make sure she's prepared, that I'm not going to hurt her. That's the last fucking thing I want to do to this woman. "You ready for this, sweetheart?"

"Yes..."

Her response comes breathy and full of the same need tightening my entire body. I can't hold back any longer. I drag my hips back and drive into her hard, shifting her entire body up the elegant piece of furniture. She tightens around my cock, and I grip her hip with one hand. Holding her steady, I capture her cheek in the other one to align my lips with hers as I plunge into her.

Every bow of her hips to meet mine cements me farther inside her and makes me crave her even more. Our bodies move together fluidly, rolling and arching and slapping together. Gasps and moans of pleasure fill the space between us, and I lean down to graze my lips across hers.

"You feel so fucking good, Jack." I shift my hips slightly to alter the angle, and the head of my cock drags against her G-spot, catching ever so slightly. "Fuck."

She squeezes her eyes closed on a sharp inhale of breath. "Oh, right there. Right *there*!"

I pull my hips back and drive into her again. And again. Over and over. Hard and fast. Relentlessly. Twisting up with each thrust to ensure maximum contact. But it still isn't enough. I drag her to the edge of the chaise and lift her left thigh to throw her leg over my shoulder, opening her even more and giving me the ability to plunge even deeper.

A strangled groan falls from her lips, and she claws at the fabric beneath her, finally wrapping her hands around the base of the lounge to ground herself.

Leaning forward, I catch her mouth with mine, gliding my tongue along hers and ramming into her like the madman I've felt like since the moment I saw her.

Primal.

Frantic.

Desperate.

Unlike anything I've ever experienced with any other woman I've been with. But from the first time our eyes met across that bar, I had to have her, and it's every bit as good as I knew it would be.

I slip my hand between us and find her clit, rolling it as thrust after thrust bottoms out deep inside her.

"Yes, like that. I'm gonna—" She gasps, bowing further into me. "I'm gonna come."

My lips ghosting across hers softly, I cup her cheek. "I want you to come for me again, Jack. I want to see your face. Feel your cunt tightening around me. I want you to squirt all over me. I want my fucking cock and this couch soaked."

"Oh, good God. Fuck!" She tosses her head back and forth frantically, like something is building in her that she's trying hard to contain. Like she's fighting it instead of embracing what it will be.

"Let it go, Jack."

"No!" She squeezes her eyes tightly, looking almost pained to be holding it in. "I can't—"

"*Look at me!*"

Her eyes flutter open at my command, the amber blazing back at me.

"Let. It. Go." I roll my hips, driving up into her and twisting her clit between my fingers.

Her mouth falls open as her body spasms. Nails claw at the chaise. Her pussy ripples along my cock, grasping and clenching, instinctively trying to draw out my release.

Fuck, she's beautiful when she comes.

The absolute definition and picture of ecstasy.

Everything I've always wanted to find in a woman, even if it's only for one night. At least it's one I'll remember.

She reaches up and clings to me like I'm the only thing keeping her grounded, and I know exactly how she feels. The low burn starts at the base of my spine and explodes through my body, her pussy finally succeeding. I come hard and long, emptying myself into her and gritting my teeth so hard that I almost crack them.

"Jesus...fuck..."

Jack sags back onto the chaise, and I drop on top of her, supporting myself on one elbow so my weight doesn't crush her. I nuzzle my face against her warm, damp skin and drag my tongue along the elegant column of her neck up to her ear to pull the lobe between my lips and suck.

Her body twitches under me, her cunt squeezing again around my still-hard cock, and she groans and rolls slightly away from me. "Fuck. Are you trying to kill me?"

I chuckle and release her ear, then cup her cheek and turn her face toward me. A tiny grin plays on her lips, and I kiss her gently.

"It would be a good way to go."

JACK

GROANING, I squeeze my eyes closed tighter against the light streaming in from the windows and roll away from it, straight into a wall of hot, hard flesh. A deep, rumbling, satisfied groan comes from immediately next to me. It takes a second for my brain to process and remember what happened last night.

Oh, God.

But my body doesn't need time to remember. There's no way it could ever forget. Everything aches in the best way possible, a physical reminder of how incredible the last several hours have been with this man.

I never knew one night could be so all-consuming.

Intense.

Passionate.

Emotional.

Draining to both my body and my soul.

The entire experience with Nolan has been nothing short of magical, a sexy, very not-for-children fairy tale. Though, he is *not* the Prince Charming we're told about in the stories read to us before bed. He's the handsome, debonaire villain, the one who lures you in with beautiful words and promises of everything you could ever want. Only, unlike those men, Nolan actually delivers.

The man is phenomenal. I was absolutely correct to think he would be. He doesn't just talk a big game; he plays it—far too well. I feel it through every fiber of my being, every cell in my body. He's left his mark—permanently. All in one damn night.

A strong arm wraps around my waist and drags me across the bed until my face is buried against Nolan's hard chest. That scent that has become so familiar fills every breath. He tightens his grip on me, squeezing me close. "Going somewhere?"

Yes.

No.

Fuck...

I should be.

Mom and Dad are no doubt losing their shit by now and probably have the entire city of Chicago looking for me. Knowing the lengths they'll go to in order to protect me from all the perceived threats—internal and external—they're probably tearing apart every bar, restaurant, and hotel for any sign I've been there. I should go before they find me, before they do something truly rash in order to locate me and bring me home.

I should.

But this is too nice, too comfortable, too...*everything* for me to even consider getting up at this moment to face the fallout of what I did. It's so much easier to snuggle into Nolan and pretend the outside world doesn't exist for a few more minutes.

Just a few more.

That's what I keep telling myself as I let myself relax into Nolan, into the moment. He drags his fingertips down my exposed spine, and a shudder rolls through me, making me press myself against him even harder, my legs wrapped around his thigh, pussy pressed to his warm skin.

"No." I shake my head. "Not yet."

But this can't last much longer; I can't hide here forever, no matter how badly I may want to. No matter how much I've enjoyed this, how much I actually *like* Nolan.

He presses a kiss to the top of my head, groans, and reaches to the side of the bed to grab his phone from the nightstand. His fingers fly over it quickly, then he tosses it back down and sets those Caribbean-blue eyes on me. "I don't know about you, but I'm fucking famished."

My stomach growls in response, and I giggle at the unladylike sound. "Yeah, I could definitely eat."

We didn't even come up for air last night, let alone stop for any sort of sustenance. And I am definitely feeling it this morning as my body is begging to be fed.

That sexy half-grin spreads across his lips, and he twists a strand of my hair around his finger. "Well, I just ordered us breakfast, but I'm in the mood for something else."

Heat flickers deep in his eyes, a flame of lust that can only be extinguished one way.

Oh, hell.

After the way he made me come like a damn

faucet in the hallway last night and worked me over again and again in this massive suite, I don't know if I can take another full-on oral assault from Nolan.

My cheeks heat at the mere memory, and my thighs clench around his involuntarily against the throbbing of my clit.

His grin grows even wider. "Thinking about the hallway?"

I duck my head to hide my embarrassment, trying to bury it against his shoulder, but he rolls me onto my back and settles over me, pinning my hands above my head and staring down at me with mischief gleaming in his gaze.

I release a little groan. "It's just so...I don't know. Embarrassing."

He stills, his brow furrowing slightly. "Why is coming embarrassing?" He shifts my wrists into one hand and drags the other slowly down my body to my thigh, leaving goosebumps in its wake. He cups my exposed pussy in his large hand. "Nothing about what we did last night should embarrass you, Jack. Trust me, a woman squirting like that is the hottest fucking thing in the world."

My entire body heats with his touch and the memories.

The elevator...

The hallway...

The chaise in the living room...

Then the bed in here...

How many times did *we have sex?*

Four?

Five?

I lost count of how many orgasms I had before the clock even ticked over past midnight, and I don't even want to think about how Nolan got so damn good at knowing a woman's body. Or why there was an unopened box of condoms waiting for us on the bedside table last night.

He shifts his hand and gently slips a finger inside me. I moan and tighten my thighs against his hand. Heat spreads from my core upward into my belly, a longing for something I can't possibly need again when I still ache from last night.

A low, deep chuckle rumbles in his chest. "Sensitive this morning, sweetheart?"

"Uh-huh."

He releases my wrists and slowly shifts down until his head is directly between my legs, the heat of his breath making my body clench, and he throws back the covers, exposing me for the first time in broad daylight. I try to squeeze my thighs closed against his hand again, but he spreads them carefully, like he's opening something precious and to be appreciated.

"Nothing I haven't already seen, sweetheart. You're fucking beautiful, and I promise I'll be gentle on you."

I laugh, shaking my head. "I don't think you even know what gentle means."

He gapes in mock offense and then grins at me. "Well, now, I feel like I have to prove myself."

"Oh, you don't have to prove *anything*. You more than proved everything you needed to last night."

Far more than once.

He smirks and dips his head to glide his tongue ever so gently across my pussy. I groan at the sensation against my overly sensitive flesh. My abraded thighs from his beard last night still open more, though, and my hips buck up to meet him. The low rumble of satisfaction he issues vibrates through my thighs as he slowly spreads me open even more and glides his tongue through me again. So tenderly. So slowly. It's almost worse than the way he tortured me in the elevator. Not enough to really get me off. Just enough to toy with me. And he's proving his point.

Very well.

I dig my fingers into his hair and tug on it until he looks up at me

He lifts his head and licks his wet lips. "What's the matter, Jack?"

"You know..." I let out breathlessly.

One of his dark eyebrows wings up. "Do I?"

I nod vigorously. "Need more."

He drops his head again and flicks his tongue across my clit, sending a jolt of pleasure through me that makes my hips fly up. "I'll tell you what, Jack. Since you're so sensitive this morning..." He pushes up from between my legs and rolls onto his back next to me. Reclining against the headboard, he rests his hands behind his head. His entire perfect body is on display, spread out across the pristine white sheets. "You come take what you need. You're in control this morning."

"Really?" I throw my leg over his hips, straddling him and taking his cock in my hand to stroke it, brushing my thumb across the pre-cum leaking from the head. "You're ready to give up control?"

After how he dominated me in ways I didn't even know I needed all night, the last thing I ever expected was for him to make an offer like this.

He nods once. "Really." His palm lifts to my cheek and his thumb glides over my lips. "I want to see you ride my cock and take what you need from me."

What I need from him...

Nolan has already more than given me what I was seeking out of our time together—an escape from *life* and its stressful realities. I had my wild night of fun, and really, I should go before someone figures out where I am. But I can't leave him like this. Not when my body is craving more, even as it aches from how much we've already done.

He reaches over to the bedside table, grabs a condom, and hands it to me, watching as I tear it open and slowly unroll it down his length, his jaw clenched.

I shift across his lap to line up his cock with my pussy, then slowly ease onto him. A heavy breath slips from my lips as my body stretches to accommodate how big he is, especially in this position.

"Fuck, Jack..." His hands fall down to my hips, and he squeezes hard. "You have no idea how good you feel."

If it's anything like what he does to me, then I do.

I grip the headboard for leverage, taking a moment to adjust to his size, and just revel in him filling me. His fingers tighten, a silent urging for me to move, and I slowly push myself up until just the head of his cock remains inside me, then sink back down.

Any soreness I was experiencing when I woke disappears on a cloud of lust now enveloping my body. Nolan clasps my hips and starts helping me move.

Slow and steady.

Nothing frantic or hurried like we were each time last night.

He's being careful not to hurt me, no matter how badly he may want to move harder and faster. His body tenses each time I squeeze my pussy around him, trying to restrain that desire. He clenches his jaw, the muscles of his neck straining as I ride him languidly, taking everything I want at my own pace.

I lean forward slightly so I can grind my clit down against his pelvis and get the friction I need so badly to push myself over the edge. In this position, it won't take me long to come, and given the way Nolan's entire body is straining under me, it doesn't look like he will, either.

Nolan's hooded gaze locked with mine, I press my lips to his, letting my tongue glide against his. His responding groan goes straight to my core, making me tighten around him. One of his strong hands clasps the back of my head to hold me in place, and he consumes my mouth while I take his cock.

Our pace increases slightly, and he braces his feet against the mattress and begins to thrust up to meet each downward motion, driving himself even deeper.

I pull back and gasp, squeezing my eyes closed against the sensations consuming me. His hands find my breasts, and he flicks his fingers across my nipples, then grabs one and twists. The sharp jolt of pain mixing with pleasure makes my body twitch and squeeze around his cock even tighter.

"Yeah, just like that, Jack." He practically growls the words. "*Fuck* me. *Take* it."

Unlike the many I've already had, this orgasm builds slowly, a low warmth spreading from between my legs up through my belly and out to my limbs before it finally crescendos, stealing my ability to breathe. My movements falter, but Nolan keeps pushing up into me, keeps me going, grinding his pelvis against mine until he groans and finds his own release.

I sag against him, pressing my forehead to his as our breaths mingle. He kisses me slowly and deeply, sweetly, and wraps his arms around me, tugging me tightly against him.

Our chests move in unison, hearts racing together until they finally start to slow. I can't even remember being so relaxed, so content, so *happy*. And with a man I don't even know...

A sharp knock sounds at the door, and I reluctantly pull back from him slightly.

He winks at me. "Excellent timing, Jack."

I chuckle against his lips and kiss him again. "It certainly was."

5

ISAAC

Jack leans back in her chair, the plush white robe wrapped around her falling open enough for me to almost completely see her bare breasts as well as flashes of her pretty pink cunt every time she shifts positions.

She brings a strawberry to her mouth and closes her lips around it, groaning slightly when it hits her lips. "Gosh, these are good."

I adjust my growing semi in my boxers, where I sit at the table across from her and pop one into my mouth, chasing it with a sip of champagne. "They are." My gaze drifts from her perfect lips down over her chest and to her crossed legs. "You know, you don't need to wear that robe."

A bright laugh slips from her mouth, amusement

glinting in her amber gaze. "Oh, yes, I do." She motions to the spread on the table—a sampling of a dozen breakfast foods since I had no idea what she would want and had *other* things in mind when I was placing the order. "I need to eat, and if I'm naked, that will never happen."

I issue a low chuckle and cut a piece of steak on my plate. "I do have *some* self-control, you know."

One of her brows rises playfully. "Oh, really?"

"Yes." I take my bite and chew, watching her watch me. Swallowing, I lean forward and rest my elbows on the table. "You think I'd survive law school if I didn't?"

She taps her fork against her cheek playfully. "That's true, but I can see you being held in contempt quite a few times during your career."

Beautiful smartass.

I bark out a laugh and sit back in my chair, taking a sip of my champagne. "I feel like I should maybe be offended by that."

Her thin shoulders rise and fall nonchalantly. "It isn't meant as an insult. You just don't seem like the type who is likely to back down from anything, especially if you're arguing a case for a client or something like that." She stabs a piece of potato with her fork and points it at me. "That silver tongue of yours is going to get you in trouble."

Examining the woman who has managed to captivate me so wholly in such a short amount of time, I grin. "I think it already has."

This was supposed to be one night. One night of fun before I go back to New Orleans and step into the role I was born to take. One night to be free from expectations and the weight of being who I am. One night to be anyone else but Isaac Hawke.

Only, I don't want it to end.

I don't want to finish this breakfast, check out, and go back to my damn condo and then the airport tomorrow to fly away from Chicago like none of this ever happened. I don't want to forget Jack.

Not that I ever could.

It's the best I've felt in a long time. The freest. The happiest. And it isn't just because I'm getting my dick wet with a beautiful woman. There's just something about her that lights up from the inside, and it somehow does the same for me.

Jack takes a sip of her champagne, slowly uncrossing and recrossing her legs, being sure to flash her swollen pussy at me. I smirk at her and glance at the half-empty plates on the table.

We managed to mow through a lot of what I ordered, which shouldn't be a surprise given the way we worked up an appetite. Now that our bellies are full, I'm not ready for her to rush out of here.

I need more time with her.

Need to feel her against me.

Just need more of *her.*

I refill my flute and motion for Jack to tilt hers toward me so I can do the same for her. The bubbles rush up the side, and I pull back the bottle just in time to stop it from overflowing. I push to my feet, my drink in one hand, the bottle in the other, and motion toward the bedroom.

"Come."

Her dark brows rise. "I think I've come as much as I physically can for a while."

I chuckle and make my way over to her, leaning down to press a kiss to the top of her head. "I have something else in mind."

Narrowing her eyes on me, she climbs from the chair with her glass. "No funny business."

Juggling the bottle, I hold up three fingers. "Scout's honor."

She playfully pushes at my bare chest, laughing. "You were *not* a boy scout."

"Sure was." I incline my head for her to walk in front of me back to the bedroom. "Made it to Eagle Scout."

She scoffs, glancing over her shoulder at me and pausing at the door. "I don't believe you."

"I'm serious. I thought it would look good on a law school application."

"Wow." Her eyes widen, and she giggles. "Aren't you just full of secrets?"

She has no idea...

I brush past her with a wink and lead her into the ensuite, setting down the bottle and my flute on the counter. She follows slowly, lip between her teeth, watching me and trying to figure out where I'm going with this.

"Don't look so scared." I grin at her and reach for the small pink bottle on the counter. "We're taking a bubble bath."

Her brow furrows like she can't quite comprehend what I just said, and her gaze drifts over to the large soaking tub. "A bath?"

"Mmm hmm." I plug the drain and crank on the hot water while Jack leans against the counter, looking at me like I'm batshit crazy. "A nice, hot, bubble bath."

"You don't seem like the type who takes bubble baths."

I bark out a laugh that echoes off the tile and slowly pour in the bubble mixture, swishing the water with my hand. "I'm not. I was probably five the last time I took one. But for you, I'll make an exception."

She pulls her bottom lip back between her teeth, shifting on her bare feet and glancing toward the door. "Actually...I probably should get going..."

Get going?

Something slowly tightens around my chest, making it hard to breathe. A feeling I haven't experienced before, a longing for someone who is standing right in front of me.

I push to my feet and make my way over to her slowly, not wanting to make her any more uneasy than she clearly already is. "You have big plans today? Somewhere to be?"

She glances up at me, twisting her lips. "No. Not really, but this seems a little..."

"A little what?"

Her slender shoulders rise and fall. "I don't know...intimate?"

"Intimate?" I close the distance between us, pinning her against the counter with my body and taking her face between my hands. "I've literally been inside you, almost non-stop, for the last twelve hours. You came down my fucking throat in that hallway last night. And taking a *bath* with me is too intimate?"

I raise a brow at her in challenge, daring her to consider my words and still stand by her statement. The smile pulls at the corners of her lips until she can't fight it anymore.

"Well, when you put it like that..."

I lean into her and stop my lips just short of hers. "Stay with me another night. My flight doesn't leave until almost noon tomorrow. I'm not ready for you to leave yet."

That admission awakens something deep in my gut, pulls at something dormant, something I've refused to even consider before this moment. If she says no, if she decides to walk away from this room and me today, there's absolutely *nothing* I can do about it. I can't *force* her to stay if she doesn't want to, and I never would try, no matter how much I want it.

This was supposed to be one night, and that one night is long over. It just doesn't *feel* like *this* is.

I brush my lips over hers gently. A request. An invitation. A plea for her to give me, give *us* more time —one more night. She issues a tiny little groan from somewhere deep in her chest and wraps her arms around my neck, clinging to me like she needs me as much as I need her, when I had been so afraid she would try to push me away.

Our kiss deepens, our bodies pressed together tightly, almost begging for more, but the sound of the water running behind me forces me to drag my head away from hers. I glance back to ensure the tub isn't overflowing yet, then turn to Jack and ask with my gaze what I can't seem to voice again.

Please stay.

Her amber orbs burn into mine for a moment before she peeks over my shoulder and offers a lop-sided grin. "We should probably get in there before it overflows."

Thank fuck.

JACK

BETWEEN THE WARM, bubbly water completely enveloping me and Nolan's firm body at my back, I could easily drift off and never return to the stress and turmoil of the life that awaits me outside this bathroom, this hotel, this man's arms.

That's why I stayed when the rational side of me screamed that I had to get out of here. This all has just felt too good to be true. I don't get to have things as beautiful as Nolan, a man as kind, caring, generous, and passionate. I get told what to do, have orders barked at me, have my entire life controlled under the pretense of "protecting me." Staying here means my world is likely going to shit.

I'll have to face the consequences when I return, but I can't even consider them right now. That would ruin this incredible moment with this incredible man.

Whose name I don't even know.

But it's better this way. Safe for both of us. It makes it easier to walk away tomorrow when he heads back to wherever home is for him and I return to Mom and Dad and everything being their daughter entails.

Nolan's lips press behind my ear, and he tightens his arms around me. "Where did you just go?"

I shake my head, trying to clear the last remnants of the thoughts that could derail the enjoyment I'll get from every moment we get to spend together. "Nowhere. I'm here." I turn my head and look at him, offering what I hope is a genuine-looking smile. "Nowhere else I'd rather be."

The blue of his eyes darkens, and he reaches a hand out of the water to brush his wet fingers across my lips. "Why do I think you're lying about at least half that answer?"

Shit.

Apparently, I suck at hiding how I'm really feeling. That's something I should try to remember so I don't fuck up with Mom and Dad when I face their inquisition tomorrow.

"That's a lawyer skill, isn't it? Being able to tell when someone is lying on the stand?"

Nolan releases a deep chuckle that jostles my body and swishes the surrounding water. "Yes, and I'm happy to see I have it even though I haven't actually practiced as an attorney yet, only appeared in court under my internships."

"I have no doubt you're going to be a brilliant lawyer." I sigh and lean into his touch. "And I'm sorry. I wasn't trying to lie, just...thinking about something I have to deal with when we return to the real world."

Somehow, we keep finding ourselves thinking about and discussing the very things we're trying to forget. Maybe it's just human nature to want to share those types of struggles and thoughts with someone you're intimate with, but it's something we need to stop doing. It will make walking away tomorrow so much harder.

"Hmm." He presses his lips together. "The real world." A heavy sigh heaves his chest. "I don't want to think about that right now. It will come soon enough. The moment I step onto that plane, I'm heading straight for it. Let's just pretend it doesn't exist as long as we're in this room."

"That sounds like an amazing plan."

He dips his head and presses his lips to mine slowly, but it isn't the heated, sexual type of kiss he's been giving me since we stepped into that elevator last night. This one seems to be sealing his promise that what we're doing here now is just for us, that we won't let the real world encroach on whatever we have for these two days. That it's okay to just let go and *be*.

And I'm more than willing to go along with him on this wild ride.

He breaks the kiss, and I settle back against his chest, drifting my hands through the endless bubbles filling the tub, enjoying the lack of any rush and the peaceful quiet of the room, broken only by the soft sound of Nolan breathing.

His chest rises and falls gently, and he slowly drags his fingertips up and down my arms in a way that forces my eyes closed and makes my body relax even more.

After the physical exertion of the last twelve hours, this was much needed. The soreness melts away, and a comfortable silence settles around us, both of us enjoying the peaceful warmth and our quieted minds now that we've agreed to keep everything else out of *this*.

For two people who barely know each other, it

shouldn't be this *easy* to *feel* this content, this secure, this...happy. Yet, somehow, it just *is*.

I almost don't want to move, but I force my eyes open so I can find my glass of champagne on the ledge beside the tub and tip it back, taking a sip of the effervescent liquid. Nolan shifts, doing the same, and I glance back at him as I replace mine.

He offers me a grin and slides a hand across my stomach, stopping just above the place where my body has come to crave his touch. I turn and press my lips to his slowly, sliding my tongue along and requesting entry. He takes me into his mouth, tangling his own slick tongue with mine, both tasting like sweet champagne and need.

His cock grows against my ass, and a tiny moan slips from my lips against his. The strong arm around me tightens, and he shifts under me slightly before he pulls his head back, locking his warm eyes with mine.

"Are you trying to have *sex* with me in the tub, Jack?" He rolls his hips under me, making sure I'm aware of what I'm doing to him but doesn't move his hand down between my legs. "Isn't that a bit *intimate?*"

Humor dances in his gaze and plays on his lips at his use of my own words against me.

Smug asshole.

I only said it because this was too good, too real, but now I want to drown in that feeling, in him, in everything we can have until we go our separate ways tomorrow. But before I do that, I want him to suffer the same torture I did last night, waiting for his touch, his mouth, his cock; I want revenge.

Biting my bottom lip beneath my teeth, I bat my eyelashes, doing my best to look innocent and hide my true intent even as I intentionally brush my hand against his hard cock where it strains between us before reaching for my glass again. He bites back a little strangled groan.

Bringing my champagne to my lips, I pause before I take a sip. "I'm telling you—that smart mouth of yours is going to get you in trouble someday, Nolan."

He raises a dark eyebrow at me. "Someday?"

I nod, taking another drink.

A low chuckle rumbles his body beneath me. "Oh, Jack, it already has. Many, many times." His hand tightens on my hip, and he moves his in a way that makes his cock brush against my thigh suggestively. "And it got you here with me, didn't it? That's *definitely* trouble."

He has no idea.

If any of the people undoubtedly out looking for me now found me here, Nolan would find himself on the wrong side of a war he never knew he was getting dragged into.

One he can never win.

That's why this time tomorrow, I'll be gone, and he'll be a happy memory. Until then, I'm going to play, and I'm going to enjoy the hell out of it.

6

JACK

It doesn't take much convincing to make Nolan desperate to get out of the bathtub—just a few well-placed brushes of my hand against his cock and pressing my lips to his again, letting my tongue languidly tangle with his.

He groans into my mouth and drags me out of the water to my feet, setting me on the bathmat so he can climb over the porcelain edge and pull me into his arms again. His hard length presses against my belly, and my pussy clenches, the very recent memory of how incredible he feels inside me making me crave even more. But there's something else I need to do first. Something I've been longing to do since the moment he first touched me. Something he's distracted me from doing with that silver tongue and skilled hands.

Nolan kisses me deeply, but when he shifts his hand down to move between my legs, I nudge it away and back him up to the counter. His brow furrows in question. By way of answering, I dip my head to his chest, then lower to his stomach, and lick a droplet of water trickling down over his abs, from just above his strained cock up over his nipple, adding a little bite to it.

He issues a low growl of appreciation, his hips shifting toward me, seeking more that I'm certainly willing to give him. I take his hard length in my hand and lower myself to my knees. Lust blazes across his blue eyes, staring down at me with such intensity, I might spontaneously combust right here on the spot.

That look, like he wants to devour me, only intensifies as I take his cock between my lips and slowly suck it into my mouth.

"Sweet fuuuuck..." His head drops back, his eyes close, neck muscles straining, and his hands bury themselves in my hair, tangling in the strands.

His warm flesh sits on my tongue, heavy, hard, ready to explode already, and I can't help but think about what he did to me in the elevator. How he toyed with me, left me hanging until we got into the hallway, and he could destroy me in front of the camera and anyone who might happen to walk out of their room.

It might have been hot as fuck, but it was also frustrating and pure agony before it became the most explosive orgasm I've ever had in my life. And it makes me want to do the exact same to the man who did it to me.

Never taking my eyes off him, I slowly pull back my head until only the tip of his cock remains between my lips, then softly lick around it, concentrating on that hypersensitive spot just on the underside of the ridge. His hands tighten in my hair, and he tugs on it sharply. His head drops so he can watch me torture him.

Seeing him like this, barely restraining himself, his control about to slip, makes a sense of power surge through my veins that only spurs me on more. I release him from my mouth and tighten my grip around his dick, lifting it so I can lick the underside from the base all the way to the tip as slowly as possible.

Nolan clenches his jaw. A muscle there tics, and his legs begin to shake as I toy with him, licking and kissing and stroking his flesh but not taking him back into my mouth like he so desperately wants me to.

"Fuck, Jack..." He jerks on my hair until my eyes meet his again. "This is a dangerous game you're playing."

Don't I know it.

This entire weekend has been dangerous—for him, for me, for my heart. And I don't want it to end.

Not yet.

One more night.

Tomorrow, I'll deal with the fallout.

I smile and swirl my tongue around the head, pushing into the little slit and lapping up the pre-cum seeping out of it.

Nolan issues a low, deep growl again and rolls his hips forward against my mouth, urging me to continue to take him deeply and finish him off. I pause for a moment, his cock pushing between my lips, begging me to open for him and take a moment to gaze up at the pure, raw beauty of this man.

With all the hard muscles of his body tense and straining, he might as well be a Greek god looking down at me instead of a real-life man.

And I can't wait to completely undo him.

Locking my gaze with his hooded, lust-soaked one, I suck him down, angling my head to take him all the way until my lips press to the base of his dick.

He makes a strangled choking sound and pushes a fraction of an inch deeper, down my throat so far it feels like he reaches my damn stomach. I swallow around him and glide my tongue along the underside of his hard length, slowly pulling myself back. His hips roll forward, and he shoves himself into my mouth again and again. The iron grip on my hair gets impossibly tighter, and he fucks my mouth like he's chasing something more than an orgasm.

Maybe he is.

Maybe we *both* are.

Because this feeling with him is addictive.

Terrifying and ethereal all at the same time.

And he feels it, too. With every thrust of his hips, twist of his fingers in my hair, grunt and groan from deep in his chest, he gives himself to me.

He jerks hard on my hair, forcing my eyes up, then he grits his teeth and shoves into my mouth one final time, emptying his load down my waiting throat without looking away for a second, like he's claiming me, making me his.

I swallow around his cock, the salty flavor of his release making my pussy clench to have it there. Nolan tugs my head back, pulling his wet dick free, and stares down at me for a moment, both of us panting and trying to catch our breaths. Only the desire hasn't subsided from his gaze, and his cock is still hard as a fucking rock, jutting out in front of my face.

His right hand slips from my hair and cups my cheek worshipfully, like he can't believe I'm here on my knees for him. Then he brushes his thumb over my lips as his tongue darts out and licks his own.

I'd give anything to know what he's thinking at this moment, what he's seeing as he looks down at me. The blue of his eyes darkens to almost midnight, and he reaches for me and drags me up against him, slamming his lips to mine in a brutal, demanding kiss.

Far from relieving whatever was pent up inside

him, it seems what just happened has only spurred him on more, made him need something else, the same thing my body yearns for. I press my thighs together against the throb between them and moan into his lips, just as hungry and desperate as he is.

Pulling his mouth from mine, he grips my chin and squeezes it firmly. "Are you on birth control?"

It takes a second for his question to process through my lust-hazed brain. I can't even seem to form words. Instead, I nod as much as his grip allows.

His eyes darken even more. "Is there any reason I shouldn't fuck you bare right now?"

Oh, God...

I shake my head. "No."

"Good, me either." He pushes off the counter and spins me around so I'm facing it, then wraps his arm around my chest and drags me back against him, his cock pressed between my ass cheeks. He grips my chin and twists my head until our eyes meet. "I'm going to fuck you hard, Jack. So hard you might not be able to walk to leave tomorrow, but I don't know how long I'm going to last with the feeling of your bare cunt around my cock. If it's anything like what your mouth felt like, this is going to be fucking fast."

I don't even care.

It could be five seconds or five hours—I just need him inside me.

Nolan releases me and pushes on my back until my breasts hit the cool marble counter, then kicks open my legs with his foot and drags his cock through my dripping center. "Jesus Christ, Jack...are you ever not wet for me?"

I shake my head. "No."

"Thank fuck."

He grips my hips and rams into me in one aggressive thrust that rocks me forward. I brace my hands against the counter, and he wraps my hair around one wrist and jerks my head back until I can see us in the mirror.

"Watch, Jack. Watch me fuck you. Watch yourself come all over my cock."

God, yes!

Nolan unleashed like this is so natural, so beautiful, so *him*. He isn't bound by the expectations of his family or his career. That carefully practiced restraint and the polished, professional persona he uses for the courtroom falls away with every drive of his hips.

"God, you're so fucking hot and tight."

I squeeze around him, and he drags his cock back and plunges into me again. The muscles in his neck strain, and he clenches his jaw as he sets a mind-bending rhythm, hammering in and out of me.

His hips piston relentlessly. His body so tense it might snap. His grip on my hair just painful enough to feel fucking incredible.

Without any barrier between us, the heat of his cock and the way the head drags against just the right spot inside me make my legs shake.

"Touch yourself, Jack. Make yourself come."

"Oh, fuck..." The words tumble from my open mouth because as soon as I touch myself, this will be over. I'll be done for. As it stands, I'm barely hanging on, clinging to the edge of that cliff, waiting to fall over.

I brace myself with my left hand against the mirror and reach down with my right to find my clit. Nolan gives a sharp tug on my hair and continues to plow into me, urging me without words to do what he's commanded.

There's no way to deny him.

I barely brush my finger against the apex of my thighs and jerk on his dick—the sensation almost too much to handle with my body primed and ready after our bath and having his cock in my mouth. I roll my finger around that sensitive spot as he plunges into me with a force that rocks me forward with each thrust.

My eyes drift closed, and he jerks hard on my hair again.

"Eyes open!" His gaze locks with mine in the mirror and holds it there. "Fucking watch!"

I couldn't look away even if I wanted to. His eyes hold mine like a tractor beam, pulling me to him, forcing me to see him become an animal force, using my body to find his release as I find mine again.

This orgasm detonates like a nuclear bomb—my entire body searing with heat in one instant before it explodes. Pleasure tingles my limbs and jerks me off my feet. My legs sag, and my pussy clenches around his cock.

"Fuuuuck..." He grits out the word and pumps into me impossibly harder. "Yes, come, Jack. Milk my fucking cock."

And I do.

It hardens even more inside me as he drives into me one last time, then empties himself, his hot cum filling a spot I didn't know was empty inside, before he collapses on top of me.

He releases my hair and slowly kisses up my back to my neck. One of his hands slides across the front of my throat, and he tilts my head back until his lips find my ear. "I'm not letting you leave tomorrow without getting your name. Your *real* one. You're not walking away without giving me that."

ISAAC

FOR THE FIRST time in what seems like forever, I wake slowly, not jerked from slumber by a blaring alarm alerting me to get my ass moving—to class, to my internship, to work, to whatever else is on my plate every damn day.

My brain comes back online at a leisurely pace— the sound of busy Monroe Street below seeping in lightly through the window, the low hum of the AC unit in the room, my own breath. I allow myself to sag farther into the mattress and pillow—satiated and content after another incredible night with Jack. Better than even our first together.

I didn't even know that was possible, but somehow, it's true.

She's a complete stranger, yet, somehow, she's reached into my soul and found a part of me I wasn't even aware was there. A part that wants *more*. More than mindless, meaningless sex that only satiates me for so long. More than working myself until I'm dead on my feet. More than what's expected of me. More than how I've been living the last twenty-five years. Jack somehow calms the unrest constantly plaguing me, gives me a glimmer of a vision of what life *could* be like with the right person.

And the more time we spend together, the more times I take her and we come together physically, the more convinced I become that the right person is *her*. That we met for a reason, despite the fact that I'm supposed to be leaving.

I can't get enough of this woman. Even now, after we've spent two days doing nothing but enjoying each other, my hard cock still strains, seeking her out, wanting what only she can give me again.

And again, and again, and again.

It was only supposed to be one night, but now, I can't just walk away. Maybe it was stupid to think I ever could. From the moment I saw her, I *knew* it. I *felt* something different. And now that I've experienced it, I won't let her leave without getting her *real* name and number. Some way to find her.

What the hell am I going to do?

I can't stay in Chicago, not when everyone is depending on me to go home, but maybe I can come back to see her in a few weeks once I've helped Dad catch up and things settle down a bit.

That doesn't solve the problem long term, though.

Fuck. Long-term? Am I really thinking that word about a girl I've known for less than forty-eight hours?

I need time to think, to figure this out, to find a way we could maybe make whatever this is work. But right now, all I need is Jack—again. Rolling onto my side, I reach over to her side of the bed, only instead of finding her warm, lush body and smooth skin, my hand hits the empty sheets.

It's still early, and a huge part of me wants to just go back asleep, but my aching dick has other ideas. Ones that require I find Jack wherever she is in the suite.

I force open my eyes against the pale morning light and push myself up, scanning the bedroom. "Jack?"

Only eerie silence comes back as a response.

My gut tightening, I throw back the covers, practically leap from the bed, and pad into the empty bathroom, the empty living room, the empty conference room. All the places I enjoyed that woman over the last two days.

All empty.

"What the fuck?"

I stalk back into the bedroom and survey it again. My eyes land on a small piece of paper sitting on the pillow where she's laid her head the last few days when we weren't fucking every which way on every other surface of the suite.

Shit.

Acid churns in my stomach as I rush over and pick it up with a shaky hand.

That was fun!
- Jack

"Fuck."

She's gone.

I let the note flutter to the bed and drop my hand on the sheets where she fell asleep only a few hours ago. Not fully cold yet. She couldn't have left that long ago. There's still time to catch her.

God willing.

I scramble around the bed and grab the hotel phone to dial the concierge desk.

"Palmer House concierge, this is Austin. How can I help you?"

Shit.

This would be a hell of a lot less awkward if Chris were manning the desk. At least he knows me and wouldn't balk at my request.

"Hi. My girlfriend just left our room and forgot something she needs for the day. She's not answering her cell phone. Would you be able to tell me if you saw her leave yet or if she's still down there in the lobby?"

"Oh, certainly, sir." The phone jostles slightly, like he's moving. "Can you describe her?"

Fuck if I can't.

Her face. Her hair. Her body.

Everything about her has been seared into my memories.

Branded there.

Something I'll never be able to forget even if I tried.

"About five-three. Curvy. Long red hair. Wearing a black dress with an open back and heels."

"Oh, yes, sir. She came down a few moments ago."

Relief floods my chest. "Is she still here?"

"I'm uncertain, sir. I don't see her from where I am, but as you know, we have quite a large lobby."

Shit. Shit. Shit.

All that hope vanishes in a millisecond, replaced by a sense of doom that makes it almost impossible to take a breath. "I'm on my way down. Can you go check the rest of the lobby, and if you see her, stop her?"

"I'll see what I can do, sir."

I drop the phone into the cradle and race to my pants and shirt, where they still lie strewn on the floor of the living room from the first night we spent here. The scent of her perfume and cum still lingers on the fabric, filling my lungs while I jerk on my pants, tug up the zipper, and throw my arms into my shirt sleeves. There isn't any time to worry about how disheveled I might look, and I don't give a fuck what anyone might think of me as I rush out the door, not even bothering with shoes.

Time isn't on my side. Apparently, neither is fate. To dangle a woman like Jack in front of me and then steal her away without so much as a *chance*.

I rush to the elevator and press the call button, fumbling with my shirt buttons as I pace the hallway. My hands shake, making it impossible to slip the tiny white buttons through the small holes.

Fuck this.

Giving up on the shirt, I slam my finger against the call button repeatedly, but it doesn't bring the elevator any faster. All it does is make me more nervous and angrier.

That was fun?

Really?

How could she just walk away after this weekend? Am I fucking crazy to believe there was something more between us, that this could be more?

Every second I wait is agony, and by the time the ding sounds and the doors slide open, I'm practically vibrating in place. I hustle inside and punch the button for the lobby, then lean back against the wall, staring at the spot I worked her over on our first night together.

Christ, that was hot.

She *was hot.*

And so much more.

I started to lose myself to that woman—a realization that has me scrubbing my hands over my face and issuing a frustrated groan.

What kind of pussy have I suddenly become? Chasing after a damn woman?

It's illogical. It's *insane.* It's nothing I am. Yet, I'm barefoot, in wrinkled pants, a mis-buttoned shirt, in the elevator of one of the nicest hotels in the city, about to step into that lobby and try to chase down a woman I don't even know.

The numbers descend so slowly that it feels like an hour before I finally reach the main floor and the doors slide open. A tiny taste of what I gave her that night by making her wait. I rush out, scanning for familiar red hair.

"Sir?" A man approaches with "Austin" on his name tag.

"Did you find her?"

He shakes his head. "I'm sorry, sir. She must have exited the hotel."

"Shit." I race toward the front doors, bare feet pounding on expensive marble. "Shit. Shit. Shit."

I probably look like a fucking lunatic right now, and I don't even care.

In the end, it doesn't matter. I'm leaving in a few hours, and the likelihood of me ever coming back to the Palmer House or ever seeing any of these people again is slim to none. When I land in New Orleans to take my rightful place in the Hawke empire, I'll worry about appearances. Now, all I can worry about is *her.*

I push past the bronze Peacock doors and catch a glimpse of the red hair I had wrapped around my hand last night while I took her from behind. She stands at the curb next to the open door of a dark SUV, just outside the main sliding exterior doors of the hotel.

Thank God.

She hasn't left yet. There's still time. Time to say whatever the fuck it is I'm going to in order to try to get her to stay, or at least to give me a way to see her again.

Running through the small front foyer toward the sliding doors that lead out to Monroe Street, I keep my eyes locked on her, silently willing her not to move.

Don't get in that fucking car, Jack!

She slides into the back seat just as the hotel doors open for me. Her car door closes with a deafening slam that reverberates through my chest where I stand only feet away.

Even through the darkly tinted windows, I can feel

her eyes on me, igniting every cell of my body, reawakening and rekindling everything I've experienced over the weekend. The things I wasn't sure were real. But she doesn't roll down the window. Doesn't open the door. Does nothing to acknowledge the fact that I'm standing right here, waiting for her.

The SUV peels away from the curb, taking her with it on a sharp sound that makes me wince.

I stand stunned for a moment, trying to process what's happening before my body gets with the fucking program, and I take off, running down the cool, dirty sidewalk of Monroe Street, my heart stuck in my throat.

It's a fruitless effort. Any other time of day, this street would be bustling, full of cars and cabs and buses and people, but with the light traffic this early in the morning, the SUV builds speed and disappears around a corner, taking Jack with it before I ever get within twenty feet of it again.

I jerk to a stop at the corner, chest heaving, breath coming out in hard pants.

What the hell just happened?

She fucking left.

Without a word to me. Without giving me her name. Knowing there will be no way for us to ever see each other again.

The reality hits me harder than any of the guys at the boxing gym back home ever have, squarely in the gut, making me double over and squeeze my eyes closed against the desire to vomit all over the Chicago sidewalk.

She's gone.

And I have no fucking way to find her.

 I HOPE you enjoyed *Night Hawke,* the prequel to Isaac and Jack's story which continues in **Ruthless Hawke,** the first novel in the Hawke Family Second Generation Series!

Get RUTHLESS HAWKE: book s2read.com/RuthlessHawke

You can also binge the entire original Hawke Family Series! Download book one, *Savage Collision,* for FREE right now here: https://Book Hip.com/MSGZCQK

ABOUT THE AUTHOR

Gwyn McNamee is an attorney, writer, wife, and mother (to one human baby and two fur babies). Originally from the Midwest, Gwyn relocated to her husband's home town of Las Vegas in 2015 and is enjoying her respite from the cold and snow. Gwyn has been writing down her crazy stories and ideas for years and finally decided to share them with the world. She loves to write stories with a bit of suspense and action mingled with romance and heat.

When she isn't either writing or voraciously devouring any books she can get her hands on, Gwyn is busy adding to her tattoo collection, golfing, and stirring up trouble with her perfect mix of sweetness and sarcasm (usually while wearing heels).

Gwyn loves to hear from her readers. Here is where you can find her:

Website: http://www.gwynmcnamee.com/

Facebook: https://www.facebook.com/AuthorGwynMcNamee/

FB Reader Group: https://www.facebook.com/groups/1667380963540655/

Newsletter: www.gwynmcnamee.com/newsletter

Twitter: https://twitter.com/GwynMcNamee

Instagram: https://www.instagram.com/gwynmcnamee

Bookbub: https://www.bookbub.com/authors/gwynmcnamee

Tiktok: https://www.tiktok.com/@authorgwynmcnamee

OTHER WORKS BY GWYN MCNAMEE

Billionaires of New Orleans:
The Hawke Family Series

Savage Collision (The Hawke Family - Book One)

He's everything she didn't know she wanted. She's everything he thought he could never have.

The last thing I expect when I walk into The Hawkeye Club is to fall head over heels in lust. It's supposed to be a rescue mission. I have to get my baby sister off the pole, into some clothes, and out of the grasp of the pussy peddler who somehow manipulated her into stripping. But the moment I see Savage Hawke and verbally spar with him, my ability to remain rational flies out the window and my libido takes center stage. I've never wanted a relationship—my time is better spent focusing on taking down the scum running this city—but what I want and what I need are apparently two different things.

Danika Eriksson storms into my office in her high heels and on her high horse. Her holier-than-thou attitude and accusations should offend me, but instead, I can't get her out of my head or my heart. Her incomparable drive, take-no prisoners attitude, and blatant honesty captivate me and hold me prisoner. I should steer clear, but my self-preservation instinct is apparently dead—which is exactly what our relationship will be once she knows everything. It's only a matter of time.

The truth doesn't always set you free. Sometimes, it just royally screws you.

AVAILABLE AT ALL RETAILERS:

books2read.com/SavageCollision

Tortured Skye (The Hawke Family - Book Two)

She's always been off-limits. He's always just out of reach.

Falling in love with Gabe Anderson was as easy as breathing. Fighting my feelings for my brother's best friend was agonizingly hard. I never imagined giving in to my desire for him would cause such a destructive ripple effect. That kiss was my grasp at a lifeline—something, anything to hold me steady in my crumbling life. Now, I have to suffer with the fallout while trying to convince him it's all worth the consequences.

Guilt overwhelms me—over what I've done, the lives I've taken, and more than anything, over my feelings for Skye Hawke. Craving my best friend's little sister is insanely self-destructive. It never should have happened, but since the moment she kissed me, I haven't been able to get her out of my mind. If I take what I want, I risk losing everything. If I don't, I'll lose her and a piece of myself. The raging storm threatening to rain down on the city is nothing compared to the one that will come from my decision.

Love can be torture, but sometimes, love is the only thing that can save you.

AVAILABLE AT ALL RETAILERS:

Books2read.com/Tortured-Skye

Stone Sober (The Hawke Family - Book Three)

She's innocent and sweet. He's dark and depraved.

Stone Hawke is precisely the kind of man women are warned about— handsome, intelligent, arrogant, and intricately entangled with some dangerous people. I should stay away, but he manages to strip my soul bare with just a look and dominates my thoughts. Bad decisions are in my past. My life is (mostly) on track, even if it is no longer the one to medical school. I can't allow myself to cave to the fierce pull and ardent attraction I feel toward the youngest Hawke.

Nora Eriksson is off-limits, and not just because she's my brother's employee and sister-in-law. Despite the fact she's stripping at The Hawkeye Club, she has an innocent and pure heart. Normally, the only thing that appeals to me about innocence is the opportunity to taint it. But not when it comes to Nora. I can't expose her to the filth permeating my life. There are too many things I can't control, things completely out of my hands. She doesn't deserve any of it, but the power she holds over me is stronger than any addiction.

The hardest battles we fight are often with ourselves, but

only through defeating our own demons can we find true peace.

AVAILABLE AT ALL RETAILERS:

books2read.com/StoneSober

Building Storm (The Hawke Family - Book Four)

She hasn't been living. He's looking for a way to forget it all.

My life went up in flames. All I'm left with is my daughter and ashes. The simple act of breathing is so excruciating, there are days I wish I could stop altogether. So I have no business being at the party, and I definitely shouldn't be in the arms of the handsome stranger. When his lips meet mine, he breathes life into me for the first time since the day the inferno disintegrated my world. But loving again isn't in the cards, and there are even greater dangers to face than trying to keep Landon McCabe out of my heart.

Running is my only option. I have to get away from Chicago and the betrayal that shattered my world. I need a new life-one without attachments. The vibrancy of New Orleans convinces me it's possible to start over. Yet in all the excitement of a new city, it's Storm Hawke's dark, sad beauty that draws me in. She isn't looking for love, and we both need a hot, sweaty release without feelings getting involved. But even the best laid plans fail, and life can leave you burned.

Love can build, and love can destroy. But in the end, love is what raises you from the ashes.

AVAILABLE AT ALL RETAILERS:

books2read.com/BuildingStorm

Tainted Saint (The Hawke Family - Book Five)

He's searching for absolution. She wants her happily ever after.

Solomon Clarke goes by Saint, though he's anything but. After lusting for him from afar, the masquerade party affords me the anonymity to pursue that attraction without worrying about the fall-out of hooking-up with the bouncer from the Hawkeye Club. From the second he lays his eyes and hands on me, I'm helpless to resist him. Even burying myself in a dangerous investigation can't erase the memory of our combustible connection and one night together. The only problem... he has no idea who I am.

Caroline Brooks thinks I don't see her watching me, the way her eyes rake over me with appreciation. But I've noticed, and the party is the perfect opportunity to unleash the desire I've kept reined in for so damn long. It also sets off a series of events no one sees coming. Events that leave those I love hurting because of my failures. While the guilt eats away at my soul, Caroline continues to weigh on my heart. That woman may be the death of me, but oh, what a way to go.

Life isn't always clean, and sometimes, it takes a saint to do the dirty work.

Steele Resolve (The Hawke Family - Book Six)

For one man, power is king. For the other, loyalty reigns.

Mob boss Luca "Steele" Abello isn't just dangerous—he's lethal. A master manipulator, liar, and user, no one should trust a word that comes out of his mouth. Yet, I can't get him out of my head. The time we spent together before I knew his true identity is seared into my brain. His touch. His voice. They haunt my every waking hour and occupy my dreams. So does my guilt. I'm literally sleeping with the enemy and betraying the only family I've ever had. When I come clean, it will be the end of me.

Byron Harris is a distraction I can't afford. I never should have let it go beyond that first night, but I couldn't stay away. Even when I learned who he was, when the *only* option was to end things, I kept going back, risking his life and mine to continue our indiscretion. The truth of what I am could get us both killed, but being with the man who's such an integral part of the Hawke family is even more terrifying. The only people I've ever cared about are on opposing sides, and I'm the rift that could end their friendship forever.

Love is a battlefield isn't just a saying. For some, it's a reality.

books2read.com/SteeleResolve

You can find information on the rest of Gwyn's books on her website:

www.gwynmcnamee.com

Printed in Great Britain
by Amazon

56969470R00066